FRANK 'N' STAN

M. P. ROBERTSON

F

FRANCES LINCOLN
CHILDREN'S BOOKS

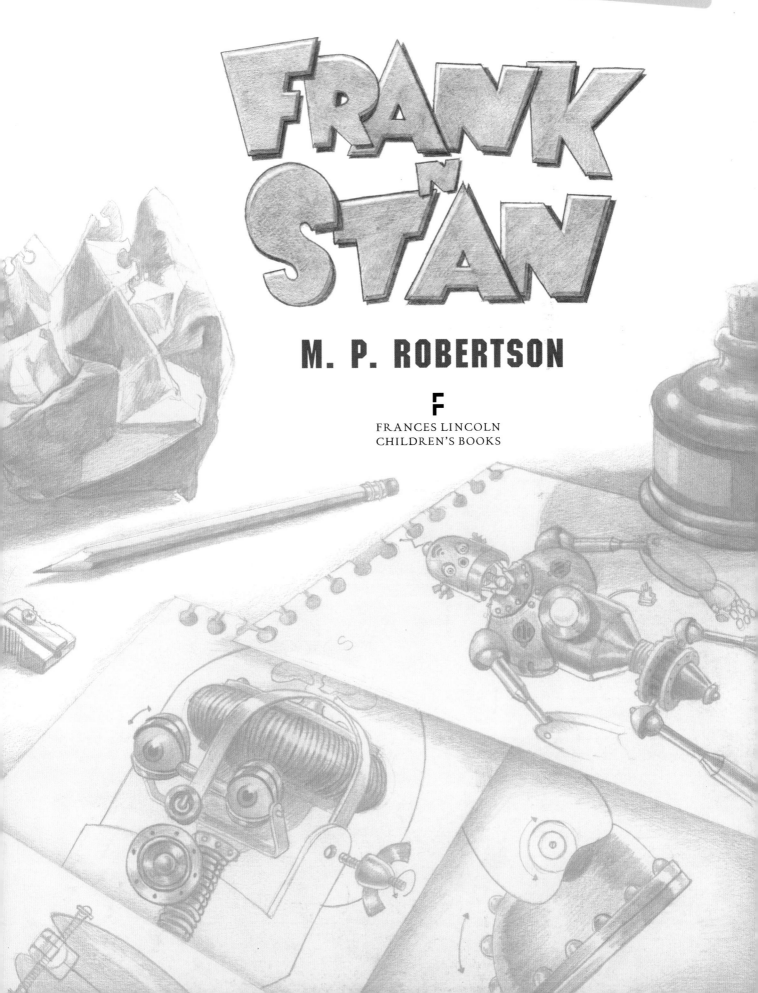

Franklin P. Shelley often asked his mother if he could have a brother or sister but she just said,

But Frank knew what to do. If his mother wouldn't make him a brother, then he would build his own. He would call him Stan.

JANETTA OTTER-BARRY BOOKS

First published in Great Britain and in the USA in 2012 by
Frances Lincoln Children's Books,
74-77 White Lion Street, London, N1 9PF
www.franceslincoln.com

First paperback published in Great Britain in 2013

A catalogue record for this book is available from the British Library

ISBN 978-1-84780-160-9

Illustrated with pen and watercolour

Printed in China

9 8 7 6 5 4 3 2

Find out more about M.P. Robertson's books at www.mprobertson.com

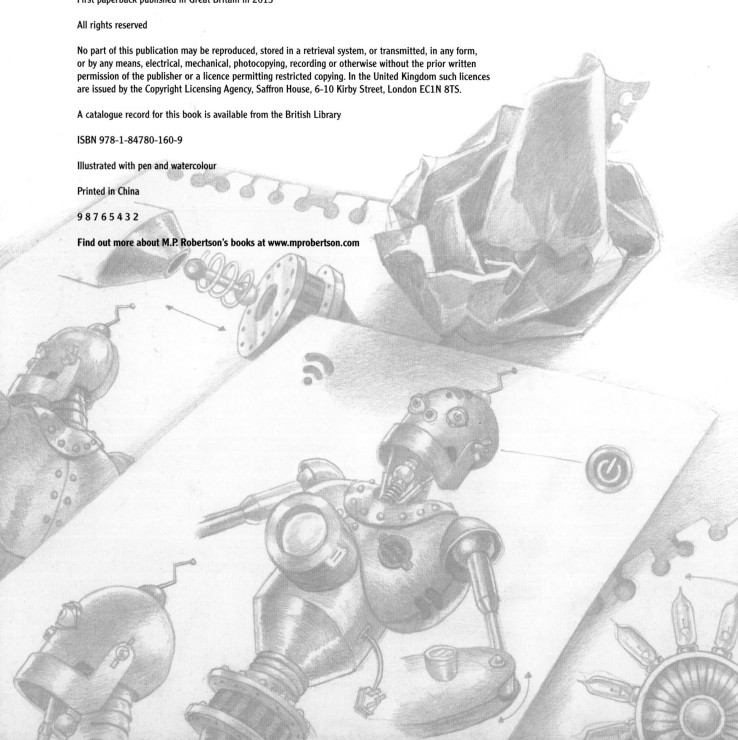

Plans needed to be made...

Parts needed
to be found.

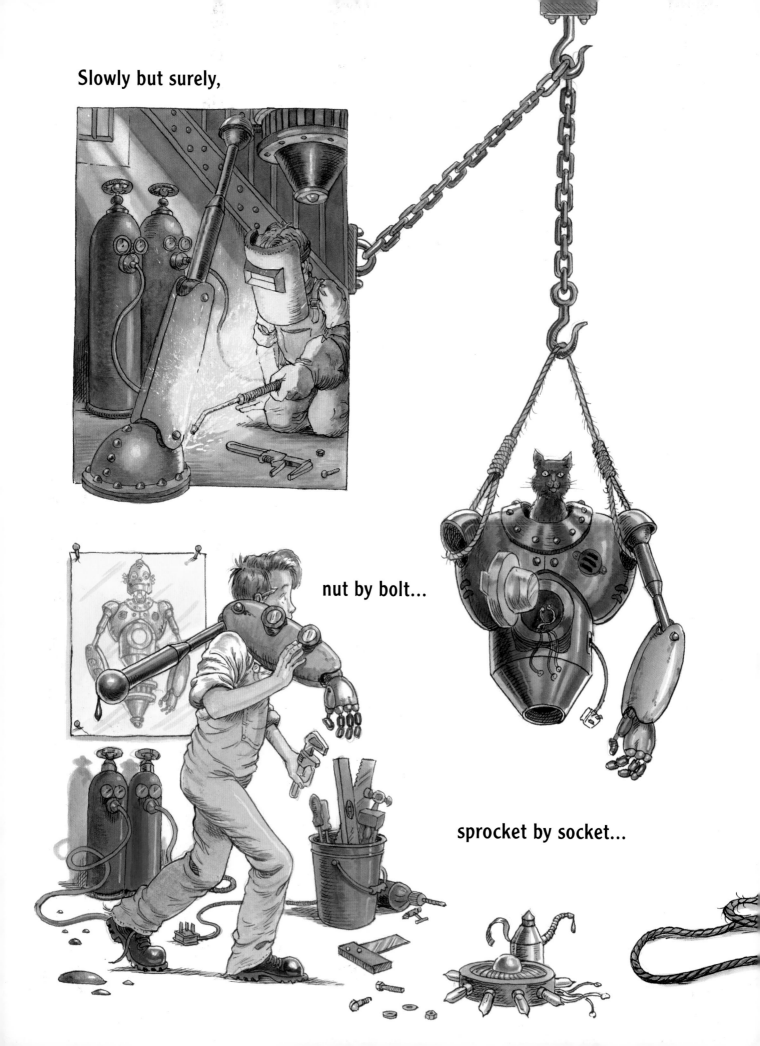

Slowly but surely,

nut by bolt...

sprocket by socket...

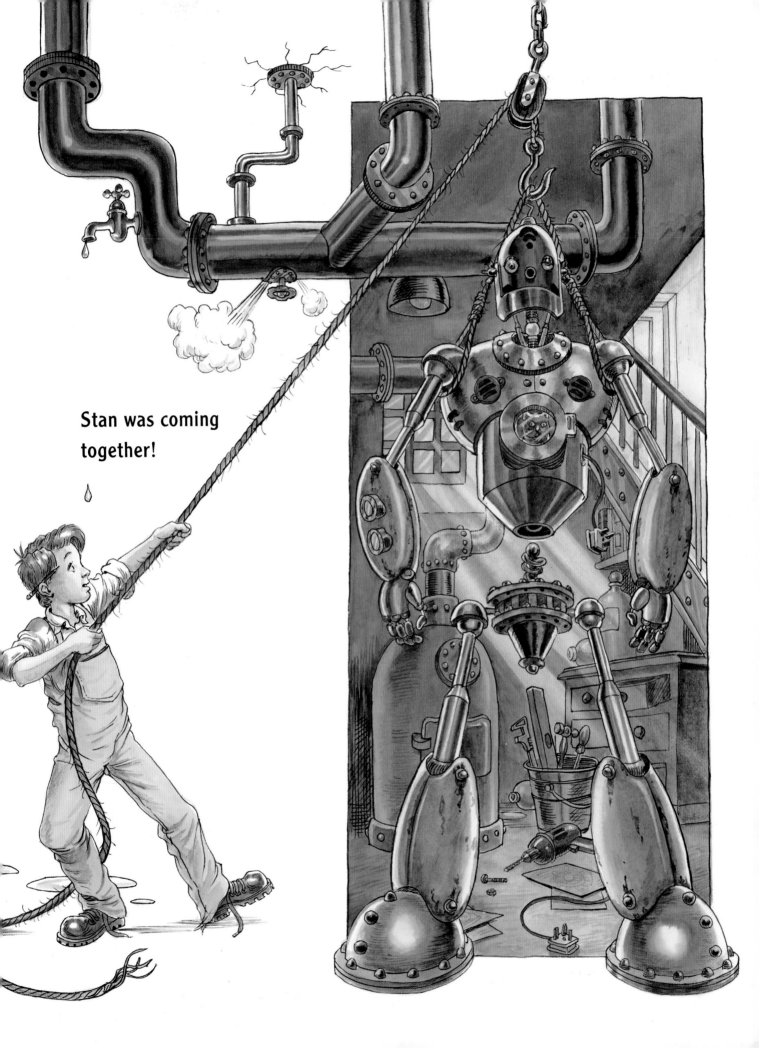

Stan was coming together!

At last, all that was left to do was charge Stan's battery...

and switch him on.

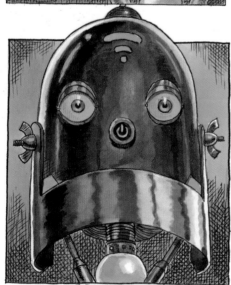

The light in his chest began to glow, then his eyes slowly creaked open.

Stan was **ALIVE!**

At first Stan was a little unsteady on his feet.

There were a few slip-ups...

and a nut or two that needed tightening.

For a baby brother,
Stan was quite unusual.

Frank's mum and dad thought
that Stan was very...

DIFFERENT!

But soon Stan was fitting in just fine.

Frank and Stan did everything together.

They built amazing things.

And made a really
BIG noise!

Then, one day, Frank's mum
gave him a little surprise...

Her name was Mary.

At first she was a bit boring...

and smelly.

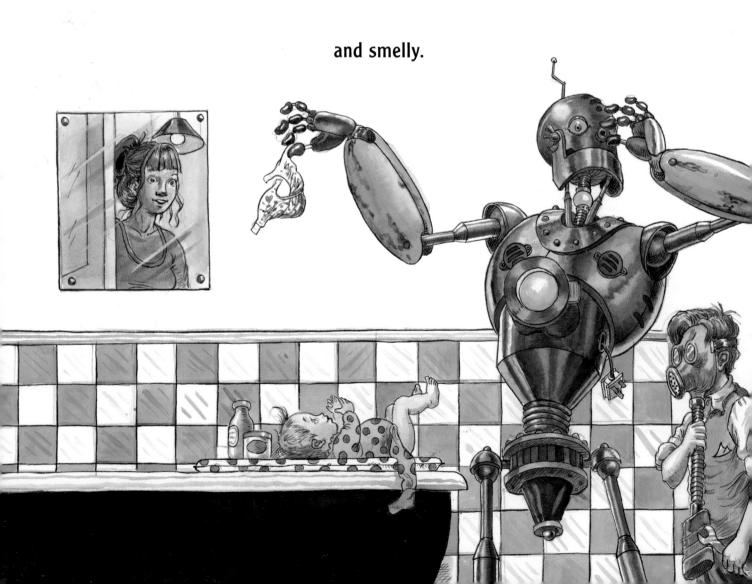

But soon she was crawling,

walking...

and climbing.

STAN

"#✳?!"

But by the time she was two, Mary
still hadn't said a single word.

As his sister got bigger, Frank started
spending more and more time with her,
and less and less time with Stan.

Stan felt left out.

One snowy evening,
he decided to leave.

He stumbled through the deep, dark woods.

He slipped across the frozen lake,

and clambered up the steep, snowy mountain.

As Stan climbed, his clanking limbs
felt heavier and heavier. And when
he reached the top he slumped down
in the freezing snow.

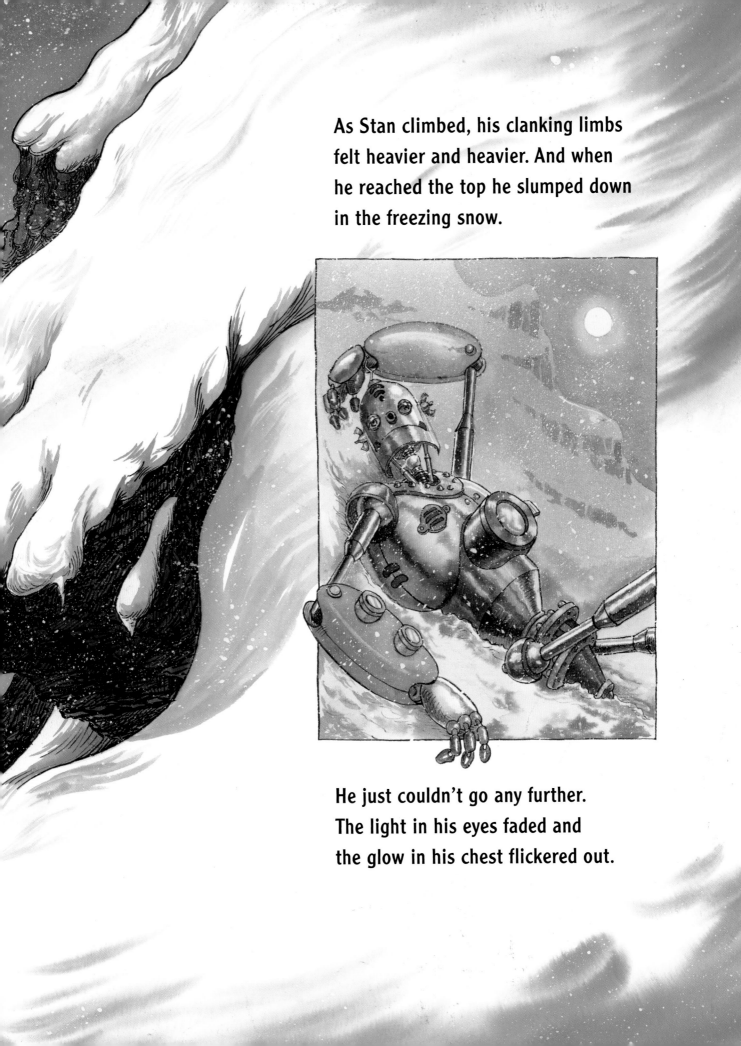

He just couldn't go any further.
The light in his eyes faded and
the glow in his chest flickered out.

In the morning, Mum missed Stan,

Dad missed Stan,

and Mary really missed Stan.

Frank knew he must find his brother
quickly, before the snow melted.

He followed Stan's tracks
into the deep, dark woods...

across the frozen lake...

and up the steep,
snowy mountain.

Snow began to fall. Frank couldn't
see Stan anywhere, but just as
he was about to give up, he saw
something glinting in the moonlight.

He shovelled away the snow
and there, lying cold and still,
was Stan.

Luckily Frank had a plan!
In his rucksack he had
a spare battery.

Stan's eyes slowly creaked open,

and Frank gave him a big 'missed you' hug.

As Stan stood up, his rusty joints creaked and groaned. But Frank had come prepared.

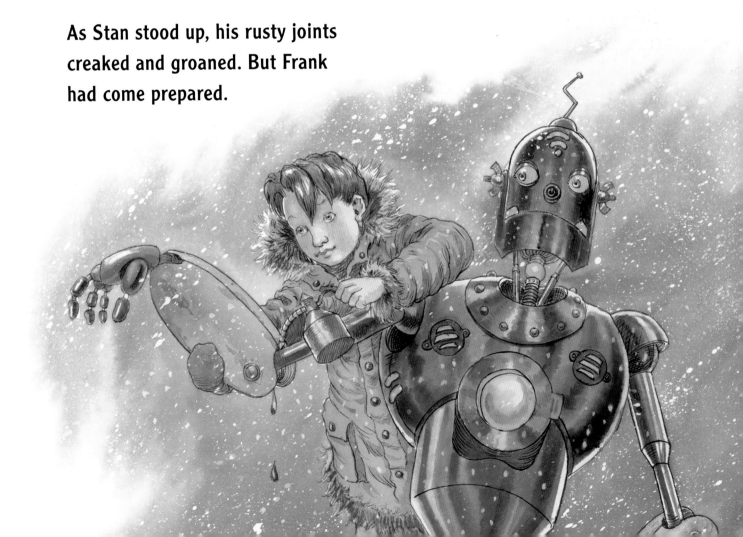

It was a lot quicker going back down the mountain!

Now Frank has a **BIG** brother and a little sister.
And when they are together they make a

GREAT, BIG, BEAUTIFUL NOISE.